Montana
The Treasure State

Marcia Amidon Lusted

PowerKiDS press™

New York

Published in 2011 by The Rosen Publishing Group, Inc.
29 East 21st Street, New York, NY 10010

First Edition

Editor: Maggie Murphy
Book Design: Greg Tucker
Photo Researcher: Jessica Gerweck

Photo Credits: Cover, pp. 11, 17, 22 (tree, flag, animal, bird), Shutterstock.com; p. 5 Zia Soleil/Getty Images; p. 7 Time & Life Pictures/Getty Images; p. 9 © Alan Majchrowicz/age fotostock; p. 13 Richard Nowitz/Getty Images; p. 15 © www.iStockphoto.com/Cynthia Baldauf; p. 19 Dr. Marli Miller/Getty Images; p. 22 (flower) Wikimedia Commons; p. 22 (Evil Knievel) John M. Heller/Getty Images; p. 22 (Jeanette Rankin) FPG/Getty Images; p. 22 (Phil Jackson) Stephen Dunn/Getty Images.

Library of Congress Cataloging-in-Publication Data

Lusted, Marcia Amidon.
  Montana : the Treasure State / Marcia Amidon Lusted. — 1st ed.
      p. cm. — (Our amazing states)
  Includes index.
  ISBN 978-1-4488-0662-1 (library binding) — ISBN 978-1-4488-0758-1 (pbk.) — ISBN 978-1-4488-0759-8 (6-pack)
  1. Montana—Juvenile literature. I. Title.
  F731.3.L87 2011
  978.6—dc22
                                    2009052002

Manufactured in the United States of America

CPSIA Compliance Information: Batch #WS10PK: For Further Information contact Rosen Publishing, New York, New York at 1-800-237-9932

Contents

Big Skies and Shining Mountains

This state is called the Treasure State, Big Sky Country, and Land of Shining Mountains. Gold and copper are mined there. Dinosaurs once **roamed** the land, and now famous people build ranches there. Where are you? You are in Montana!

Montana is located in the western part of the United States. Its northern border is Canada. Montana is found between Idaho and North Dakota and above Wyoming.

Montana was the forty-first state to join the Union. Its name comes from the Spanish word *montaña*, which means "mountain." Even though Montana is a very large state, it has a small **population**. With its tall mountains and wide open plains, Montana is a beautiful place to live or visit!

In Montana, there are many places where you can see the sky for miles (km) without any trees, buildings, or mountains getting in the way.

Gold Miners and Battles

Native Americans were the first people to live in Montana. Groups, such as the Shoshones and Blackfeet, followed the herds of buffalo across Montana's plains. The first Europeans to find Montana may have been fur trappers looking for a water **route** across the **continent**.

After the **Louisiana Purchase** in 1803, President Thomas Jefferson sent Meriwether Lewis and William Clark to **explore** the country's new territory, including Montana. When gold was discovered there in the 1860s, many more people came.

However, the Native Americans were being pushed out. In 1876, Lieutenant Colonel George A. Custer of the U.S. Army was sent to fight these tribes and keep the settlers safe.

The Battle of Little Bighorn took place from June 25 to 26, 1876. Custer's army was beaten then by thousands of Lakota and Northern Cheyenne Indians.

Rocky Mountains and Great Plains

Montana has several different kinds of land. To the west are the high tops of the Rocky Mountains, many covered with snow all year long. There are also evergreen forests and grassy valleys.

The eastern part of the state is part of the Great Plains. This land is flat and grassy with low hills, making it perfect grazing land for animals. In the southeastern corner of the state are the badlands, where **erosion** has created **canyons** and valleys.

Eastern Montana has very cold winters. However, on the other side of the Rocky Mountains, the western part of the state has cooler summers and warmer winters. Montana is also known for its blizzards, hailstorms, and earthquakes.

Here, a storm blows over the Swiftcurrent Valley, on the east side of Montana's Glacier National Park.

T. Rex and Grizzly Bears

Montana has rich forests of ponderosa pines, as well as open grasslands with willows and cottonwood trees. Wildflowers such as Indian paintbrush, fairy slipper, shooting star, and the wild rose grow there.

Dinosaurs lived in Montana millions of years ago. *Tyrannosaurus rex* and triceratops were two dinosaurs that roamed the area. Their **fossils** are still being found. Today Montana has grizzly bears and bighorn sheep in the mountains. Bison, prairie dogs, and pronghorn antelope roam the plains. Osprey fly above rivers and lakes, hunting for Montana trout and paddlefish. Montana is one of the last states to have more animals than people living there!

The grizzly bear, shown here, is Montana's state animal. The grizzly bear is one of the largest land mammals in North America.

On the Dinosaur Trail

For millions of years, dinosaurs lived in what is now Montana. **Paleontologists** learned many things about dinosaurs from the fossils found there. Today visitors can explore Montana's dinosaur history by following the Montana Dinosaur Trail.

The trail has 15 stops. Each one is a museum or a field station where paleontologists are still working to find dinosaur fossils. At the Fort Peck Field Station of Paleontology, scientists study and prepare fossil finds. At the Upper Musselshell Museum, there is a full-size **replica** of an avaceratops skeleton. This dinosaur was the first of its kind ever found. At each stop along the trail, you can learn something new about dinosaurs.

This is the jaw and tooth of a T. rex that lived between 78 and 65 million years ago. You can see this fossil at the Museum of the Rockies, in Bozeman, Montana.

What Do They Do in Montana?

Montana's open spaces and grasslands make it a great place to raise animals and grow things. Ranchers raise beef cattle, dairy cows, and sheep. Some also have llamas, emus, and ostriches! Honeybees produce 9 million pounds (4 million kg) of honey every year in Montana. Farmers grow barley, cherries, mint, and sugar beets. Many Christmas trees are also grown in Montana.

Miners in Montana dig for coal and also produce natural gas for energy. Copper, lead, gold, and platinum are still found in the mountains. With so many forests, Montana is also known for **timber**. The wood from its trees becomes lumber for building as well as things like pencils, telephone poles, and paper.

This cowgirl is rounding up calves, or baby cows, on a Montana ranch. Cowgirls and cowboys often work on ranches, but some also take part in rodeos.

The Queen City of the Rockies

Montana's capital city, Helena, is nicknamed the Queen City of the Rockies. However, this city started out as Last Chance Gulch, a small gold-mining town. After Montana became a state in 1889, Helena became the capital in 1894. The state capitol is topped with a huge copper dome, made from copper mined in the state.

In Helena's Mansion District, you can see hundreds of fancy homes built after the gold strikes of the 1860s and 1870s. You can also visit Reeder's Alley, a **restored** mining town, and see Helena's oldest house, a log cabin pioneer home. A short distance from the city, you can go sapphire hunting at the Spokane Bar Mine or visit the Elkhorn Ghost Town, built after silver was discovered nearby.

Here, you can see Montana's state capitol. Inside the building, there is a large statue of Jeannette Rankin, the first U.S. congresswoman.

Visit a Glacier

About 15,000 years ago, huge glaciers carved out the mountains that run through Montana's Glacier National Park. Glaciers are slowly moving masses of ice. The 26 smaller glaciers in Glacier National Park today are all that is left of the ancient glaciers. Because Earth is getting warmer, some scientists think that these glaciers will be gone by 2020.

Glacier National Park is also home to 1 million acres (400,000 ha) of Montana's most amazing scenery. Visitors to the park can travel the Going-to-the-Sun Road through the park's mountains. They can hike, take horseback rides, and cross-country ski in the winter. They can camp, fish, and raft down a river. Kids can view wildlife through special spotting scopes and walk across a swinging bridge.

In 1850, there were 150 glaciers in Glacier National Park. The Grinnell Glacier, shown here, is one of 26 glaciers left in the park.

Come to Montana!

If you like the outdoors and wide open spaces, then Montana is the place for you! You can hike its mountains or fish for salmon in its rivers. You could also visit a reservation and learn about Native American cultures or attend a pow-wow.

If you go to the Berkeley Pit, you can see a giant hole in the ground left by an open copper mine. You can also admire the stalactites and stalagmites in the Lewis and Clark Caverns State Park. Water dripping through limestone creates the cone-shaped rock formations under ground there. Whether you like ghost towns and dinosaurs or just want to enjoy a beautiful place, visit Montana and see why it really is the Treasure State!

Glossary

canyons (KAN-yunz) Deep, narrow valleys.

continent (KON-tuh-nent) One of Earth's seven large landmasses.

erosion (ih-ROH-zhun) The wearing away of land over time.

explore (ek-SPLOR) To travel over little-known land.

fossils (FO-sulz) The hardened remains of dead animals or plants.

Louisiana Purchase (loo-ee-zee-AN-uh PUR-chus) Land that the United States bought from France in 1803.

paleontologists (pay-lee-on-TAH-luh-jists) People who study things that lived in the past.

population (pop-yoo-LAY-shun) A group of animals or people living in the same area.

replica (REH-plih-kuh) An exact copy of something.

restored (rih-STORD) Returned to an earlier state.

roamed (ROHMD) Walked around with no special plan.

route (ROOT) The path a person takes to get somewhere.

timber (TIM-bur) Wood that is cut and used for building houses, ships, and other wooden objects.

Montana State Symbols

**State Tree
Ponderosa Pine**

**State Animal
Grizzly Bear**

State Flag

**State Bird
Western
Meadowlark**

**State Flower
Bitterroot**

State Seal

Famous People from Montana

Jeannette Rankin
(1880–1973)
Born in Missoula, MT
First U.S.
Congresswoman

Evel Knievel
(1938–2007)
Born in Butte, MT
Stunt Performer

Phil Jackson
(1945–)
Born in Deer Lodge, MT
Basketball Coach

Montana State Map

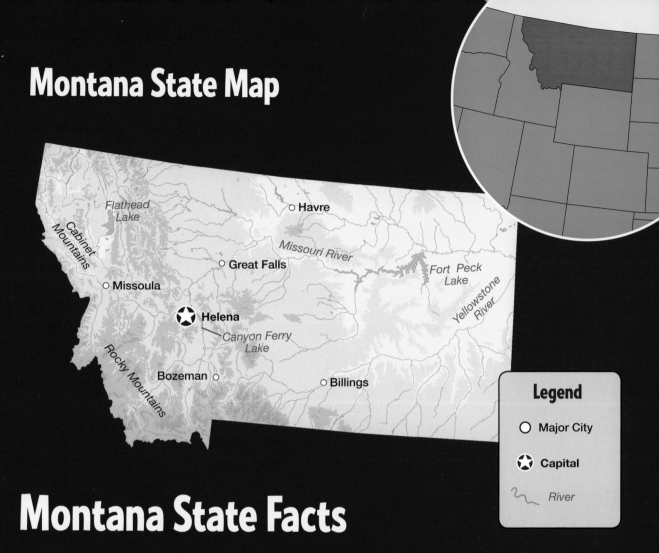

Montana State Facts

Population: About 902,195

Area: 145,552 square miles (377,000 sq km)

Motto: "Gold and Silver"

Song: "Montana," words by Charles Cohan and music
by Joseph E. Howard

Index

Web Sites

Due to the changing nature of Internet links, PowerKids Press has developed an online list of Web sites related to the subject of this book. This site is updated regularly. Please use this link to access the list:

www.powerkidslinks.com/amst/mt/